TERROR TOWN

ELF GIRL and RAVEN BOY

Also by Marcus Sedgwick
for older readers

Blood Red, Snow White
The Book of Dead Days
The Dark Flight Down
The Dark Horse
Floodland
The Foreshadowing
The Kiss of Death
Midwinterblood
Revolver
She Is Not Invisible
My Swordhand is Singing
White Crow
Witch Hill

The Raven Mysteries

Flood and Fang
Ghosts and Gadgets
Lunatics and Luck
Vampires and Volts
Magic and Mayhem
Diamonds and Doom

Elf Girl and Raven Boy

Fright Forest
Monster Mountains
Scream Sea
Dread Desert

Visit Marcus Sedgwick's website at –
www.marcussedgwick.com

TERROR TOWN

ELF GIRL and RAVEN BOY

MARCUS SEDGWICK

Illustrated by Pete Williamson

Orion
Children's Books

First published in Great Britain in 2014
by Orion Children's Books
a division of the Orion Publishing Group Ltd
Orion House
5 Upper St Martin's Lane
London WC2H 9EA
An Hachette UK Company

3 5 7 9 10 8 6 4 2

A catalogue record for this book is available from the British
Library.

ISBN 978 1 4440 0527 1

Printed in Great Britain by CPI Group (UK) Ltd,
Croydon, CRO 4YY

www.orionbooks.co.uk

For Leela

Dread
Desert

Terror Town

Creepy Caves

ONE

Raven Boy had no idea the world was so big until he set out on his adventures with Elf Girl.

They made quite a sight.

A boy with feathers in his hair, a girl in pointy-toed boots, and a scruffy little rat, all clinging to a carpet speeding through the air.

Raven Boy, for that is who it was, also clung tightly to a small glass bottle of water.

They'd risked their lives in the Dread Desert to find the oasis called the Tears of the

Moon and taken some of the precious water it contained. He really didn't fancy going back for more.

They'd sped out of the desert, across low hills and wide fields and, much sooner than they would have liked, a town came into view over the horizon. Their destination: Terror Town.

'Are you sure this is a good idea?' said
Raven Boy to Elf Girl.

'Of course it's not a good idea!' Elf Girl
replied, snappily. 'But we don't have any choice,
do we? If we're going to save the world from
the Goblin King, we need the Tears of the
Moon and the Singing Sword. And we've got
the tears, so . . .'

'So, we need the sword,' finished Raven
Boy. 'Yes, I know. I'd just rather not go to a
place called Terror Town, to look for someone
called Terrible Tim from the Horror Hotel.
That's all.'

'And you think I would?'

Elf Girl gave Raven Boy a very hard
stare, as if she was searching for fleas.

'You know how you think you got made
smarter by that genie back in the desert?'

'Yes?' said Raven Boy.

'I'm not sure it worked,' she muttered.

Then the carpet, whose name was Shona,
piped up . . .

'Passengers should prepare for landing.
Please fasten your seat belts, return your arm

rests to the upright position, open your window blinds and please note, the toilets are no longer in service.'

Raven Boy and Elf Girl really didn't like her bossy behaviour.

'What the monkey-face is she talking about?' said Elf Girl.

'Shona!' said Raven Boy. 'Don't land.'

'Passengers are reminded that they do not have operational control over take-off and landing. Passengers should . . .'

'Shona!' said Raven Boy, fiercely. 'I order you not to land. Not yet. I want you to circle the town first. Have a bit of a look around.'

'Good idea,' said Elf Girl.

'See?' Raven Boy said. 'I'm not as stupid as you think.'

'Passengers . . .'

'Just do it!' Elf Girl and Raven Boy screamed, and Shona began to sulk. But she did as she was told.

The carpet slowed, and they flew above the rooftops of Terror Town.

It was a big place. They saw all sorts of

buildings, small houses and big ones, some with several floors. There were twisting streets and one or two broad avenues. There were squares with trees and fountains, but the thing that caught their attention was a large, ancient-looking castle sitting on a hill.

'That's good,' said Raven Boy. 'Stay nice and high up. We don't want anyone to see us.'

Shona silently obeyed, though the look on her face showed how grumpy she felt about it.

'There's no one to see us,' said Elf Girl.

'Haven't you noticed?'

Raven Boy peered down. He had excellent eyesight, just like a bird, and he could see that Elf Girl was not wrong.

The streets of Terror Town seemed to be empty, or so they thought at first.

'There!' said Raven Boy. 'There's someone.'

Elf Girl saw a little old lady bustling down the street. Under one arm she carried a basket, which appeared to have food in it. She ducked under an archway and was gone.

Now Raven Boy and Elf Girl saw a few more people, but, for such a big town, it seemed rather deserted.

Raven Boy looked at Elf Girl.

Elf Girl looked at Raven Boy.

'All right,' she said, 'since you're the smarty-pants now, what do we do?'

Raven Boy tried to feel his super-smart brain working in amazingly clever ways, but he didn't feel any brighter than normal. If only Elf Girl had wished for him to be super-smart all the time, and not just said, 'I wish you weren't so *stupid* all the time.'

Then he'd know what to do.

He peered over the edge of the carpet
again, and Rat dared to walk up his back and sit
on his head to look down with him.

'Why don't we land on a roof?' Raven
Boy said. 'Land on a roof, so we have a bit of
safety. Somewhere to leave Shona.'

'Leave me?' cried Shona, surprising them
by coming out of her sulk so suddenly. 'What do
you mean, leave me?'

'Well, I'm not wandering around this
place with you rolled up over my shoulder,'
said Raven Boy. 'We'll find a quiet rooftop
and leave you there while we go and find the
Singing Sword.'

Shona started sulking again.

'There!' said Raven Boy. 'What about that one?'

He pointed, and Elf Girl nodded. He'd seen a large flat roof, not too far away.

'Good idea!' said Elf Girl. 'Maybe you're smarter than you look.'

'How smart do I look?' asked Raven Boy, but fortunately for him, Elf Girl didn't get a chance to reply.

Shona was being so sulky that she didn't make any landing announcements at all and plopped onto the roof so hard that their bottoms hurt from the landing.

'Bad carpet,' said Raven Boy. 'Very bad carpet.'

Shona just vanished, back into the fibres of the carpet, leaving them sitting on a rug on a roof, with no idea what to do next.

Two

**It's a not very well known fact
that flying carpets each have
their own personality; it's
unfortunate that Shona is as
grumpy as a tired camel.**

Raven Boy and Elf Girl glared at the carpet,
but Shona was nowhere to be seen, and they
soon realised it was hard to be cross with a rug
for long.

So they stopped.

Rat scampered around the rooftop, sniffing.

'Good idea, Rat,' said Raven Boy. 'Check
things out.'

Rat gave a little squeak.

'What next, bird boy?' asked Elf Girl.

Raven Boy looked around. The roof was high above the town. He wandered right up to the edge, and stood looking down at a drop that would have broken a piano into a thousand pieces, if a piano had happened to fall off the roof.

'OOOH' said Elf Girl.

'Hmm?'

'Not so much OOOH,' explained Elf Girl. 'More like EEEE.'

'You mean EEEP?'

'Yes, I suppose so,' said Elf Girl. 'EEEP!'

'Why EEEP?' asked Raven Boy.

'Because you're standing so close to the edge. Doesn't that make you feel the slightest bit funny?'

Raven Boy thought for a moment.

'No,' he said, 'it does not. You know I like heights. You get used to it living in tree-tops. It's not so bad, why don't you just . . . ?'

'I'm fine here,' said Elf Girl, who had decided to stay by Shona.

Raven Boy shrugged.

'Well,' he said, 'it's easy enough. What we do is shimmy down this drainpipe here, and then we'll be in the street. We can hunt about, find the sword and . . . what?'

He'd turned to look at Elf Girl, who was shaking her head.

'No way. You know what I think about climbing. And this time a fall doesn't mean getting wet, like it did in Scream Sea. This time it means getting flat. I'm not going to do it.'

She sat down on the carpet with a thump.

Raven Boy could see there was no chance of winning her over.

'Okay then,' he said. 'We'll think of something else.'

'Why don't we just get Shona to land

down there?'

'Because we're trying to be quiet, aren't we? We don't want anyone to see us. Arriving on a flying carpet is going to rather spoil that, don't you think?'

'But there's no one about!' said Elf Girl.

'There are a few people,' Raven Boy pointed out. 'And in somewhere called Terror Town, I'm not taking any chances. Look, there are pot plants on the roof.'

'Raven Boy, this is no time for gardening.'

Raven Boy sighed.

'Elf Girl, if there are pot plants, that means someone comes up here to water them, which means there must be a way down. Without climbing.'

Elf Girl stared at him again. Her eyes narrowed.

'Maybe you are smarter than you used to be.'

'Come on, get up and help me look for a way down.'

They spent ten minutes looking round the rooftop, scratching their heads, wondering

if there was an invisible door somewhere, when
finally Rat sank his teeth into Shona, the carpet,
and began to slowly drag her backwards.

There, right underneath where Shona

had landed, was a trapdoor.

Raven Boy tried the handle and the door
lifted open. Stairs led into whatever building
they were standing on top of.

'Come on then,' said Elf Girl.

'Wait,' said Raven Boy. He waved the

glass bottle that held the Tears of the Moon.
'Should we take this with us, or leave it here?'

Elf Girl considered this.

'Leave it here,' she said finally. 'Roll
Shona up, with the bottle inside to hide it.
Then leave them in the corner over there.'

Before they could blink, Shona had
reappeared.

'No one's going to roll me up and . . .'
she began, but it was too late – Raven Boy and
Elf Girl already had her wound halfway round
the bottle, and, in a moment more, they were
dragging the rolled rug over to the edge of the
roof, where they tucked her beside the low
parapet that ran around it.

'There!' said Raven Boy happily. 'We
should have thought of that before.'

'Could come in handy,' Elf Girl agreed,
and they set off through the trapdoor and down
the stairs.

It was a bright afternoon, but gloomy
inside the building.

They climbed into a dusty attic, full of
boxes and things under sheets.

'Where do you think we are?' whispered Elf Girl.

Raven Boy shook his head.

'No idea. Come on. Look, there's a door.'

Through the murk he'd spotted a way out.

Just as he reached for the doorknob, Elf Girl squeaked.

'But how do we know who lives here? It could be dangerous. Remember what this place is called!'

'There's only one way to find out, isn't there?'

Raven Boy opened the door and was gone.

Rat squeaked, and jumped off his shoulder straight onto Elf Girl's.

He squeaked again, looking desperately at Elf Girl.

'I know,' she said. 'He seems unusually brave today, doesn't he?'

She looked around the attic. It was spooky.

'Raven Boy! Wait for us!'

Elf Girl hurried after him, and Rat gave another squeak to show how he felt about the whole thing.

'Wait! Come back!' hissed Elf Girl.

She scuttled after him and could just see Raven Boy disappearing at the end of a corridor.

She rounded the corner so fast that she banged into him.

He was looking over a bannister, into a huge hall. It was totally quiet. More dustsheets

covered items of furniture, and hung over paintings.

'This is weird,' said Raven Boy.

They explored further, opening every door they came to, but no one was at home.

'The place is deserted,' said Elf Girl.

'But where did everybody go?'

'Who knows?' said Elf Girl. 'Shall we find out?'

Raven Boy had stopped looking so brave, but he nodded.

'Come on then,' he said, and they stepped out of the front door and into Terror Town.

THREE

**After miles and miles of
travelling, Elf Girl's pointy
boots aren't looking too good.
Raven Boy's coat looks just
the same as when they started
out: tatty and moth-eaten.**

Terror Town turned out to be really quite nice.
They came out onto a pretty street, with
sweet houses along each side. Very soon they
saw a short fat man with a white beard and
twinkly eyes. He said 'good afternoon' to them
and raised his hat as they passed by. Then they
met two mothers wheeling their toddlers along
in fancy-looking prams. The mothers were

chatting but nodded and smiled at Elf Girl and
Raven Boy as they went, though one of them
did peer rather rudely at Rat.

Elf Girl and Raven Boy walked on, and before too long had met at least twenty people from Terror Town. They all seemed perfectly normal and if they weren't the most chatty people ever, well, at least they didn't try to turn them into stone, like the magician in the Monster Mountains had, or run them through with a cutlass, like the pirates of Scream Sea, or, like the trolls who'd been following them from Fright Forest, try to eat them at every available chance.

All in all, Elf Girl and Raven Boy were finding it hard to work out why the place was called Terror Town.

'The houses are lovely, aren't they?' said Raven Boy. 'Almost nice enough to make me think about moving indoors.'

'Really?' said Elf Girl, sounding surprised.

'I said almost,' Raven Boy replied. 'And everyone we've met has seemed quite lovely.'

'But this place isn't called Lovely Town, is it? It's called Terror Town and we've been through enough odd things for me not to start letting my guard down now!'

'Odd?' said Raven Boy. 'That's an odd word to choose. I'd say the things we've been through to date have been deadly, dangerous and downright terrifying. If you were to ask me . . .'

'I didn't ask you,' said Elf Girl, as they came to a beautiful square, at the centre of which a fountain showered jets of water into the air. They wandered over to it, feeling thirsty.

'Have you noticed one thing?' Elf Girl said.

'What's that?' asked Raven Boy.

Rat scampered out of his pocket and hurried to the fountain.

Elf Girl waved a finger at Raven Boy.

'As perfectly nice as everything has been since we got here, no one's actually stopped to talk to us.'

That was true, Raven Boy thought. And it wasn't as if they hadn't tried.

They'd spoken to a few people, to ask if they knew where Horror Hotel was, or if they knew anyone called Terrible Tim. But no one had answered, they'd just mumbled something and hurried on their way.

'There's something funny about this place,' said Elf Girl, tilting her head under the jet of the fountain so she could drink from it.

'Maybe,' said Raven Boy. 'Or maybe everyone's just very busy.'

Elf Girl pulled her head from the fountain, and shrugged.

'Who knows?' she said.

'But what are we going to do?' asked Raven Boy. 'We need to find somewhere to sleep tonight, whatever we do. I vote for a nice high-up rooftop somewhere. Unless we can find a big enough tree, that is.'

'I don't,' said Elf Girl. 'We still have some money left and while we do, I vote for a quiet little hotel.'

'But we don't know where Horror Hotel is.'

'Not Horror Hotel. Any other hotel. The sooner the better. Look, it's getting dark.'

The sun was dipping below the rooftops, and though Raven Boy still thought a tree would be nicer to sleep in, he didn't want to upset Elf Girl.

'Someone must be able to tell us where to find a hotel,' Elf Girl said, and spotted a woman crossing the square.

'Hey! Hello!' began Elf Girl, but the woman sped away into a house on the far side of the square.

She slammed the door, and Elf Girl and
Raven Boy realised that doors were being closed
all over the square. Windows too, lots of windows,
and the shutters pulled over them.

They could hear keys turning in locks, as a few last people hurried into their homes, and shut themselves in.

The sun went down. Darkness spread across the town, here and there light poked out from the shutters.

Suddenly, a window flew open above their heads, and someone yelled.

'Hey! You down there! What do you think you're doing?'

'I don't know,' said Raven Boy. 'What should we be doing?'

'If I were you, I'd start running! Hide! They're coming!'

'Who's coming?' asked Elf Girl.

'Them!' the voice replied.

From across the square, came a low groaning, a wailing and moaning. Then a strange dragging, scraping noise, and as Elf Girl struggled to see in the dark, Raven Boy let out a terrified '**Eeep!**' because his eyesight was so super-good.

'What?' screamed Elf Girl.

'Run!' cried Raven Boy.

Elf Girl was almost crying she was so scared.

'What? What are we running from?' she sobbed, as Raven Boy tugged her hand and pulled her into a scamper.

'Zombies!' yelled Raven Boy. Rat jumped off his head and slithered into the safety of an inside pocket of his coat.

The moaning sound grew louder, and Elf Girl and Raven Boy made out one word clearly.

And that word was 'brains'.

Four

Zombies aren't fussy about what they eat – they just get excited by a moving target. It's a shame Elf Girl and Raven Boy don't know that.

'Zombies?' shouted Elf Girl.

'I know!' wailed Raven Boy.

'No, wait!' cried Elf Girl. 'Are you sure?'

'Pretty sure!'

'Raven Boy, stop running! There's no one behind us. Look!'

She grabbed Raven Boy's hand and spun him round. They were alone.

'See!' said Elf Girl. 'Are you absolutely sure you saw zombies?'

'Pretty sure,' said Raven Boy, grumpily, and he pointed back to the square, where four or five shuffling bodies appeared.

'Eeeeuk!' said Elf Girl. 'They stink.'

'So would you if you'd just climbed out of the ground!' said Raven Boy. 'Believe me now?'

'Yes, all right,' said Elf Girl. 'I believe you. Only. Only they're not so fast, are they? We don't need to run. I think we might be able to beat them at a slow amble.'

Raven Boy didn't laugh.

'Look,' he said, and pointed to the other end of the street, ahead of them, where six more zombies were shuffling towards them, moaning, 'Brains! Fresh brains!'

'Maybe they get you with numbers, not speed,' said Elf Girl. '**EEEP!**'

'You said it,' said Raven Boy. 'Try your bow! Zap 'em!'

Elf Girl gave Raven Boy a look.

'Zap 'em?'

'Just do it!' screamed Raven Boy.

Elf Girl swung her magical bow from her back and concentrated really hard, then let fly a dozen arrows at once. Real ones. They hurtled towards the zombies, every one scoring a bullseye. But the arrows went straight through, and the zombies kept shuffling.

'How can I kill them when they're already dead!'

'Good point,' said Raven Boy. 'Here's another idea. Run!'

There was an even smaller street leading off the one they were in. Raven Boy led the way and they scurried along between the gloomy buildings.

'EEEP!' cheeped Raven Boy. 'More zombies!'

They chose another street and were easily able to outrun the staggering monsters, but wherever they went, they came across more and more of them. The whole town was overrun.

'This place is terrible!' cried Raven Boy. 'Terror Town!'

'They're everywhere,' replied Elf Girl. 'What do we do?'

'Head back for the rooftop. Find Shona. Fly out of here.'

'Good plan,' said Elf Girl.

There were, however, two problems with the good plan.

The first one was that they were lost. And the second was that even when they recognised the right way to go, it was blocked by gangs of hungry zombies.

Finally, they managed to get back to the street they'd first arrived in, burst inside the building and up the stairs, taking them three at a time.

They galloped through the attic onto the roof, only to come to a horrified stop . . . because Shona, the magic flying carpet, was missing.

'Oh no!' Elf Girl screeched.

'But we left her right there!'

'She's been carpet-napped!' wailed Elf Girl.

A voice behind them said, 'Fresh brains!' and they spun round to see a dozen nasty, smelly zombies looming towards them.

'Why didn't you lock the front door?' yelled Elf Girl.

'Why didn't you?' screamed Raven Boy.

'Oh, Raven Boy,' said Elf Girl. 'I'd be so angry with you if only I wasn't so scared. I don't want to be eaten!'

'Try your bow again,' said Raven Boy.

'It's no use, you saw that.'

'Maybe you can fire something else. Like you used to, you know. Butterflies or umbrellas.'

'And how is that going to stop them?' asked Elf Girl.

'I don't know! But do something!'

All the while, the zombies were getting closer, licking their lips and muttering 'Brains are best' a lot.

'This is the slowest attack we've ever had!' said Elf Girl. 'I wish they'd just get on with it.'

'No, you don't!' said Raven Boy firmly. 'Elf Girl, how far can you jump?'

'Why do you . . . ?' began Elf Girl, but then she saw what Raven Boy was looking at. 'Oh, no! No. I won't . . . I can't . . . I . . .'

'Yes you can and yes you will,' said Raven Boy.

He was looking at the roof of the building opposite, across the narrow street. It would mean jumping.

'We have to!' shouted Raven Boy.

'I really don't want to!' said Elf Girl.

'It's that or be eaten!' screamed Raven Boy. 'Come on. We'll go together!'

He grabbed Elf Girl's hand and they sprinted towards the edge of the roof, leaping into thin air.

As they flew they just had time to notice that the street below them was full of zombies too, and then – smack! –

they landed on the roof opposite, which turned out to be very flimsy indeed.

With an enormous crash, the roof gave way, and they fell through, landing in something hot and wet.

The zombies who'd been following them toppled slowly, one by one, over the edge into the street below. Suddenly lights went on.

A old man with huge, whiskery eyebrows was glaring at them.

'You've broken my roof!' he said. 'And ruined my bath!'

Five

Travelling the world is all
very well, Raven Boy thinks,
but he'd be very happy to get
back to his forest home, and
have a bath in the little stream
near where the squirrels live.

'What were you doing on my roof?' demanded
the man.

'There are zombies!' exclaimed Raven Boy.

'Zombies?' said the man. 'Big deal!
That's no reason to fall through someone's roof!'

'We didn't mean to,' said Elf Girl. 'We
weren't on your roof. We were on the roof next
door – the zombies chased us . . .'

'. . . because someone hadn't closed the door behind us,' Raven Boy chipped in.

Elf Girl glared at him, her ears turning dangerously pink.

'And then we jumped over here and your roof wasn't very strong,' she finished.

'My roof isn't anything now!' shouted the man. 'Look at it!'

They looked guiltily at the hole above, through which they could see the night sky, stars twinkling.

'And as for my bath!' cried the man. He was so cross that his eyebrows started twitching.

'We're sorry,' said Raven Boy. 'And we're soggy. May we get out of it now?'

The man glared even harder than Elf Girl had and they took that as a good reason to climb out of his bath.

They stood dripping on the floor, wondering what to do next.

'Excuse me,' said Raven Boy as the man fussed about picking up bits of the roof. He was wearing a dressing gown and had clearly been about to get into his hot bath.

'Excuse me, but how can you think of
having a bath? Don't you know that the town is
overrun with zombies?'

'So what?'

'So what?! They're zombies. They want
to eat everything and everyone. That's what!'

'That's nothing,' said the man. He

seemed calmer now and his eyebrows were calmer too. 'Zombies are a night off.'

'A night off?' asked Elf Girl. 'Whatever does that mean?'

'It means, young lady, that when it's zombie night we can all get a bit of peace and quiet. They're harmless enough if you're not stupid enough to go outside . . .'

He glared at them once more.

'Or leave a door open and let them in after you. Zombies aren't so bad.'

'Not so bad!?' wailed Elf Girl and Raven Boy together. 'Not so bad as what?'

'Not so bad as the other things we get in Terror Town,' he said. 'Listen, I can see you two aren't from around here, maybe you'd better come downstairs, out of the cold.'

'We're awfully sorry about your roof,' said Raven Boy again.

'Do you have any money?' said the man.

'Yes,' said Raven Boy, and Elf Girl winced.

'Good, then you can give it to me to pay for the repairs. In the meantime, would you like a cup of hot chocolate? I always have one when

I've had a scare.'

'Talking of scares,' said Elf Girl, 'what are these other things you were talking about? The things that are worse than zombies?'

'My dear girl,' said the man. 'Everything is worse than zombies. Zombies are essentially very, very stupid, and very feeble. They can't punch through a wet cardboard box. So as long as we all get inside before dark, everything is just fine.'

Raven Boy blinked at this information. They headed downstairs to the kitchen where the man started warming some milk.

'Now werewolves on the other hand . . . when they come, it's a real harem-scarem night, I can tell you. And then we get ghosts once in a while. And there's vampires too, of course, and . . .'

'Wait, wait,' said Raven Boy. 'You get all these things coming here? Every night?'

'Yes. That's why they call the place Terror Town. It's fine by day, but at night, the town is cursed! Cursed!'

He waved a wooden spoon in the air dramatically, and then paused.

'Do you like half-milk and half-water?'
he asked. 'Or all milk?'

'All milk, please,' said Elf Girl.

Raven Boy blinked his beady black eyes
again.

'I'll have what she's having,' he said. 'But
listen, this curse . . . ?'

'Yes!' cried the man. 'Cursed!'

'So you weren't always called Terror Town?'

'No, we used to be called Little Nicely.'

'I see,' said Raven Boy. 'That's terrible.

But why doesn't everyone just leave?'

'And go where?' said the man. 'A few people have left. Those who had some family to go to. But most people don't have the choice. No money to start again somewhere else. So they stay here and put up with it. Night after night.'

'That's awful,' said Elf Girl. 'But you seem to have a very big house. You must be rich! Why don't you go somewhere else?'

'I couldn't do that!' said the man.

'Why not?'

'Because, dear girl, I am the Mayor of Little Nicely!'

He stood proudly, puffing out his chest and tilting his eyebrows up. Then he slumped.

'I mean Terror Town . . .'

'The Mayor?' said Elf Girl.

'What's a mayor?' asked Raven Boy.

'Still not sure you're any smarter,' said Elf Girl.

'It means I'm in charge around here,' said the Mayor.

'In that case,' said Raven Boy. 'We're very pleased to meet you. Maybe you can help us.'

'Maybe I can,' said the Mayor. 'When you've paid for my roof.'

He held out his hand and Elf Girl took the last of their money from her pockets and handed it over.

The Mayor studied the few coins with a sour look on his face.

'Oh, well,' he said. 'I like the view of the stars anyway.'

'If you're in charge,' said Raven Boy, 'then we need some help. We have to find this hotel you see, and also, our carpet has been stolen.'

'My dear boy,' said the Mayor. 'Can't you see we have enough problems of our own here, with the curse? No one's going to help you find a missing carpet.'

'But they have to!' cried Raven Boy. 'It's very important!'

'Listen here, young man,' said the Mayor. 'Nothing is as important as our curse. We have to find a way to lift it from the town.'

Elf Girl and Raven Boy thought about that. It was hard to argue with the Mayor.

'So who put this curse on your town

anyway?' asked Elf Girl, but Raven Boy had a sneaking feeling he knew what the Mayor was about to say.

His voice dropped to a whisper. 'You see, that's the terrible thing. It's him. The most terrifying creature in the whole of creation. He's known as the . . .'

'Goblin King,' said Raven Boy.

'Yes,' said the Mayor, surprised. 'How did you know?'

Elf Girl and Raven Boy looked at each other, then they looked back at the Mayor.

'I think we need to talk,' Raven Boy said.

'Very well,' said the Mayor. 'But hot chocolate first, yes?'

Six

Rat doesn't mind going on long adventures to save the world, but he had hoped the world would have more cheese in it.

Elf Girl and Raven Boy drank their hot chocolate, and although it was the yummiest thing they'd had to eat or drink in ages, they felt gloomy.

Things got worse when Elf Girl realised that if Shona was missing it meant something else had gone missing too.

'Oh, no!' cried Raven Boy.

'Oh, yes,' said Elf Girl. 'We've lost the Tears of the Moon; they were wrapped up inside her.'

'The What of the What?' the Mayor asked, so Elf Girl explained how they'd crossed Dread Desert to an oasis and taken some of its magical water.

'Why did you do that?' asked the Mayor. He was pottering around his tiny cluttered kitchen, tidying things and muttering to himself.

'Because we've been told that we need two things to defeat the Goblin King; the Tears of the Moon and the Singing Sword,' said Raven Boy. 'Only now we don't have either.'

'And you seriously intend to try and defeat the Goblin King?'

Raven Boy and Elf Girl looked at each other, just to check they still meant to try.

'Yes,' said Elf Girl.

'We do,' said Raven Boy.

The Mayor's huge whiskery eyebrows lifted so high they nearly walked off the top of his head.

'Well I never,' he said.

'And if you helped us then your town

could be called Little Nicely again, couldn't it?'
added Raven Boy. 'And not Terror Town.'

'Help?' asked the Mayor. 'Help you?'

'Why not!' said Elf Girl.

'I'll give you a million reasons why not!'
exclaimed the Mayor.

'One will do,' said Elf Girl, the tips of
her ears turning pink. Raven Boy decided to
calm things down a bit.

'Do you have any cheese?' he asked,
which earned him a blank stare from the Mayor.

'A what?' he asked.

'A small piece of cheese. Only our friend,
Rat, is very hungry too and he doesn't like hot
chocolate.'

'He doesn't like hot chocolate . . . ?'
repeated the Mayor, open-mouthed, as Rat
poked his head out from Raven Boy's pocket.

'Go on,' said Elf Girl. 'Just one reason.'

The Mayor's eyebrows crept back
towards his eyes.

'I can't,' he said eventually. 'Not one. We
ought to help each other.'

'Great!' cried Elf Girl and Raven Boy together.

The Mayor fished about in a cupboard and came back with a very large lump of cheese. Rat's eyes widened. Then he pounced, hungrily.

'So can you organise something?' Raven Boy asked, smiling as Rat ate himself stupid.

'Organise something?' asked the Mayor, sounding doubtful.

'Yes, like a search. To find our carpet and the Tears of the Moon.'

'Oh no, I couldn't do that,' said the Mayor.

'Why not?' asked Elf Girl. Raven Boy could see she was getting really frustrated, and that was never a good thing. 'I thought you said you were in charge here?'

'I am!' said the Mayor. 'Sort of. I'm in

charge of doing what Lord Socket tells me to.'

'Lord Socket?' asked Raven Boy, slapping his forehead with his hand. He was feeling confused. 'Who is Lord Socket?'

'Lord Socket is lord of the town,' said the Mayor. 'He's the master of us all. It's his place.'

'You mean he's in charge?' said Elf Girl grumpily.

'Yes,' said the Mayor.

'Then that's who we need to talk to!' she cried. 'And as soon as possible!'

'I suppose so. But we can't go anywhere tonight,' said the Mayor. 'Not with zombies on the loose. We'll have to wait till morning.'

Raven Boy and Elf Girl glanced at each other, and at Rat happily scoffing the cheese.

'I suppose we could wait till morning,' said Elf Girl.

'Yes, we could,' said Raven Boy. He turned to the Mayor. 'You don't happen to have any bread to go with that cheese, do you?'

'This isn't a hotel, you know!' said the Mayor, but he rummaged through the cupboards to find them something else to eat.

'Talking of hotels,' said Elf Girl. 'You haven't heard of a place called the Horror Hotel, have you? Or someone called Terrible Tim? We think he's got the Singing Sword, and we need it.'

'I wouldn't be much of a Mayor if I didn't know those sorts of things, would I?'

He put a bowl of apples in front of them on the table, and some bread too.

'Terrible Tim is the owner of Horror Hotel. Just round the corner from here.'

'We'll go there in the morning,' said Raven Boy. 'Before we go to see Lord Socket.'

'And then we'll be halfway to defeating the Goblin King,' cried Elf Girl, at which the Mayor's eyebrows shot back up his forehead again.

SEVEN

**Elf Girl hasn't given up
wondering what Raven Boy's
real name is; she's hoping to
catch him out one day by
asking him in his sleep.**

Next morning, Elf Girl and Raven Boy followed
the Mayor into the streets of Terror Town. They
let him go first, in case there were any zombies
left, looking for brains to eat, fresh or otherwise.

'Come along!' said the Mayor impatiently.
'It's perfectly safe now.'

They walked along the twisting streets of
Terror Town, and, in the sunshine, it was easy

to believe the place had once been called Little Nicely. Everyone they passed greeted the Mayor, and Raven Boy and Elf Girl started to feel quite important.

'Excuse me,' said Raven Boy. 'What should we call you? I mean, we can't call you Mayor, can we?'

The Mayor thought about that.

'No,' he said after a while. 'You can call me Sir.'

With that he walked on, calling 'Do hurry up!' over his shoulder.

Elf Girl shrugged at Raven Boy and they scampered after the Mayor.

'Here we are!' he announced. 'Horror Hotel.'

'Excuse me,' said Raven Boy. 'Excuse me, Sir.'

Elf Girl rolled her eyes.

'Hmm? Yes?' asked the Mayor.

'Why is it called Horror Hotel? I mean, isn't that a funny name for a hotel? Why would anyone want to stay there?'

Raven Boy wasn't too sure about these things, having lived in the treetops his whole life, apart from when he was on the forest floor, looking for mushrooms and so on. But it did seem very weird to call a place something so scary.

'Ah!' said the Mayor. 'It wasn't always called that. But when Tim took over, and decided the place needed a bit more excitement, the whole place got turned into a spooky hotel. Kind of a joke, you see?'

Raven Boy didn't see, so he shook his head.

'They put scary pictures on the walls and made the whole place really creepy. They serve scary food, like baby's fingers, which are actually sausages, and witch's eyeballs, which are actually grapes in tomato sauce.'

'Grapes in tomato sauce?' said Elf Girl, pulling a fantastically ugly face. 'Ugh!'

'Yes, business hasn't been so good lately. And then the curse came along, so now the last place anyone wants to stay is a hotel called Horror in Terror Town.'

Raven Boy looked at Elf Girl, and then at the front of the hotel. There was a large sign outside, which read 'Horror Hotel: you'll have the worst night of your life!' The front of the building was covered in cobwebs and spiders, but they were fake. A ghost was leaning out of an upstairs window, and it wasn't real either, but made from a sheet draped over a dummy.

'Can you hear something?' Raven Boy asked.

'No,' said Elf Girl.

'What? With those ears you ought to be able to hear a mouse on the moon,' said Raven Boy. 'Which would be very useful,' he added

quickly as Elf Girl glared at him.

'No,' she said. 'No, I . . . Oh yes, maybe I can . . .'

They crossed the street and as they got closer, they could definitely hear a strange noise wafting from Horror Hotel.

'Listen here, you two,' said the Mayor.

Rat squeaked but the Mayor ignored him.

'You go and sort out whatever you want to with Tim, and I'll meet you back here in a while. Then we can go to see Lord Socket.'

'Wait!' said Raven Boy.

'Hey, come back!' cried Elf Girl, but the Mayor had gone, leaving them at the door of Horror Hotel, and even though it was sunny, and even though they knew the giant spiders on the front of the building weren't real, there was something a bit scary about knocking on the door. Especially as the door knocker was made from a skeleton's hand.

'Go on,' said Raven Boy.

'Why me?' asked Elf Girl. 'And what is that noise? It sounds like someone's being tortured or something.'

'We need that sword!' said Raven Boy. 'We can't chicken out now!'

'So? You knock on the door!' said Elf Girl, folding her arms.

Raven Boy swallowed. His knees were shaking and his throat felt dry. Finally, using just his fingertips he picked up the skeleton's hand and rapped three times.

They heard a loud booming echo as the sound of the knocker rattled around the hotel. They waited a long time and nothing happened. Nothing at all.

'No one's home,' said Raven Boy. 'Let's come back later.'

'Raven Boy!' said Elf Girl sternly, and was about to grab the skeleton's hand herself, when they heard heavy footsteps approaching slowly on the other side of the door.

They heard the door being unlocked, heard a hefty bolt slide back, and then with a mighty creak, the door started to swing open.

Elf Girl grabbed Raven Boy's hand and they were both on the point of running away, when the door opened and the tiniest girl either of them had ever seen looked up at them.

'Yes?' she said.

She was even shorter than Raven Boy and Elf Girl, and neither of them was tall. She had a funny little face that made them want to giggle, all nose and squinty eyes. She tried to straighten herself as tall as she could, and put on a very serious-looking expression.

'I,' she said, 'am Terrible Tim! Welcome to Horror Hotel! Prepare to be scared!'

Raven Boy and Elf Girl fell about laughing.

EIGHT

The world is full of people with silly names; and Raven Boy and Elf Girl really ought to know better than to snigger at someone else's.

Terrible Tim was not impressed.

'What's so funny?' she asked.

Raven Boy and Elf Girl hadn't laughed so much since they'd learned in Dread Desert that a Sultan's wife is called a Sultana.

'I'm sorry!' spluttered Raven Boy. 'We're sorry! It's just that you look so serious!'

'And Tim is a boy's name!' spluttered Elf Girl.

'I am serious!' Tim declared. 'Scaring people is a serious business! And Tim is not a boy's name!'

'Yes it is!' wailed Elf Girl and Raven Boy together.

Even Rat was snickering in Raven Boy's pocket, which made his coat look as if it was vibrating.

'It is a girl's name!' yelled Tim, furiously. 'Sometimes.'

'Really?' asked Elf Girl.

'Yes,' said the strange girl in front of them. 'It's short for Timantha.'

Elf Girl tried not to snurk, which she managed, but a great snork came out of her mouth instead, even though she had her hand clamped over it.

'Timosee?' asked Raven Boy, who was having such trouble breathing that he nearly passed out on the pavement.

'Did you come here to stand on my doorstep laughing?' snapped Terrible Tim. 'I presumed you've come to stay in the hotel? We do have . . . one or two rooms free as it happens.'

Raven Boy shook his head.

'No, we don't want to stay here,' he said.

'Then good morning to you!' snapped Tim and tried to close the door.

'No, wait!' said Elf Girl. 'We've come about something else. Please don't shut the door. We need to talk to you. And by the way, what is that terrible noise?'

Only now did they see that Terrible Tim had two pieces of cotton wool, one in each ear.

'Is someone strangling cats in there?' asked Raven Boy, looking worried.

'Eh?' said Terrible Tim. 'Speak up.'

Raven Boy mimed pulling cotton wool from his ears, but Tim shook her head.

'No way,' she said. 'Not happening.'

'What is it?'

asked Elf Girl.

'You don't want to know,' said Tim, but she beckoned them inside. 'I'll show you. Then you'll wish you hadn't asked, and then, if you don't want to be guests at my hotel, you can leave me alone.'

'We might want to be guests,' said Elf Girl.

'Might we?' asked Raven Boy.

'If the Mayor won't let us sleep at his house again tonight . . . It doesn't sound like we want to be on the streets, does it?'

'You're right there,' said Tim. 'Friends of the Mayor, eh? Welcome to my hotel. If you do decide to stay, we can give you the best room in the house! It's called the Creep Suite. You'll love it.'

'Er, maybe,' said Raven Boy, but Tim didn't hear him.

The sound was getting louder as she led the way through the hotel. They passed the Revolting Restaurant and Bizarre Bar and Tim opened a door into the Lousy Lounge.

Now they recognised the sound.

It was singing. Sort of.

At first they couldn't work out where it was coming from. They were in a large room full of comfy seats and small tables. There was a stage at one side and the room was quite dark. The singing, if you could call it that, appeared to be coming from the stage.

Elf Girl and Raven Boy went closer.
The singing got louder. And worse.

'I'm so in lo-o-ove with yo-ooo-ou,' it went.
'And if you lo-o-ove me too-oo-oo,
There ain't nothing we can't do-oo-oo.'

Raven Boy looked at Elf Girl because
Elf Girl was pointing to the stage where
a chair was sitting, and on the chair was
propped ... a sword.

'The Singing Sword!'
they both cried at once.

'We've found it!' laughed
Raven Boy.

He turned to
Terrible Tim.

'You took
the sword from
the oasis of the
Tears of the Moon?'

Tim nodded.

'Can we go
outside and talk?'

she shouted. 'It's easier that way.'

The sword kept singing. It had finished one song and was starting another.

> *'Do you know how I miss you?*
> *You're so sweet it just ain't tru-oo-ue,*
> *You gotta be an angel for sure,*
> *'Cos I am always wanting mo-o-ore.'*

Tim dragged her hands down her face and opened the door to the Lousy Lounge, shutting it behind her again, as fast as she could.

She went so far as to pull one of the pieces of cotton wool out of her ear.

'Phew,' she said. 'I can't take more than a few minutes of that noise.'

'What?' asked Raven Boy. 'The singing? So why did you take the sword?'

Tim sighed.

'I thought it would help the hotel. All the spooky stuff. We had to do something, business is bad. And a top hotel should have a top attraction. I'd heard about the Singing Sword, so I went to find it. I had no end of trouble with that monster at the oasis, I can tell you. I brought the sword here, hoping it would attract customers . . .'

'It hasn't worked?' asked Elf Girl.

'Are you joking?' cried Tim. 'It never shuts up! Not for one minute. Day or night. On and on and on, singing those awful songs in that awful voice.'

Rat squeaked.

'What?' asked Elf Girl.

'Rat says he likes it,' Raven Boy explained.

Elf Girl blinked, twice.

'Everyone's entitled to their opinions,' she said.

'No they're not,' wailed Tim. 'That sword is stinky and cannot sing! It's awful! Terrible! I'd do anything to get rid of it now! I haven't had a guest staying here in weeks.'

Elf Girl and Raven Boy exchanged a long and meaningful look.

'So,' said Raven Boy to Tim. 'If we were to offer to take it off your hands . . . ?'

'What?' cried Tim. 'You're serious? Take

it! It's yours! I'll even throw in a tin of metal
polish! Just take it and tell me you're not kidding.'

'We're not kidding,' said Elf Girl. 'We've
been looking for that sword for ages. You see,
we need it to . . . '

'I don't care if you're going to slice cabbages
with it. Just have it.'

And with that, Tim ran back into the
lounge and came back holding the sword, which
she shoved into Elf Girl's arms.

'*O baby you're the one for me,*' sang the sword.

> '*And it's plain for me to see-ee-ee,*
> *That if I'm the one for yo-oo-ou,*
> *That one and one makes two-oo-oo.*'

'You're sure you want this?' asked Tim, looking a little nervous.

Elf Girl nodded.

'Yes. I mean, I think so.'

'Good! Smashing! Wonderful!' declared Tim, and before they knew what was happening, they were back on the streets of Terror Town, squinting in the bright morning sun with a sword that would not stop singing.

NINE

**Elf Girl and Raven Boy
might think the Singing
Sword is bad; but the sword is
nowhere near as annoying as
the Wailing Wardrobe, or the
Humming Hamster.**

*'I see a picture of you and me,
Underneath that big old apple tree,
I'm kissing you and you're kissing me,
Underneath that big old apple tree.'*

'Er, Mr Sword,' said Raven Boy. 'Excuse
me . . .'

But the sword wasn't listening.

Elf Girl was holding the sword at arm's length, as if it smelled slightly. They were still standing in the street, waiting for the Mayor to come back, and had been there for some time, during which the sword had only stopped singing long enough to change tunes.

> *'Why don't we take a ride?*
> *Somewhere where we can hide,*
> *A little place for us to rest,*
> *Yeah I think that's what I'd like best.'*

'Sword,' tried Raven Boy again. 'Mr Sword, Sir! Please could you be quiet? For a little while?'

Elf Girl's eyes were getting wider and wider by the minute. She was staring at the sword, unable to believe what was going on.

'Won't it ever shut up?' she whispered.

'It doesn't look like it,' said Raven Boy.

Rat meanwhile was

perched on Raven Boy's shoulder and, if it's possible for a rat to shimmy, that's just what he was doing.

'Rat's dancing,' said Elf Girl, her eyes even wider than ever.

'How is it even making any noise?' said Raven Boy. 'It doesn't have a mouth!'

The sword didn't seem to know it was being spoken about, or if it did, it didn't care. It just kept singing. And singing. And singing.

'It's not even any good!' wailed Raven Boy.

Rat squeaked crossly at this but then began bopping away once more, this time on Raven Boy's head.

'You know, when we heard about the Singing Sword, I thought it was just a name,' said Raven Boy. 'Like, because it slices through the air so quickly or something, when it's chopping people's heads off.'

Elf Girl frowned.

'And this thing is supposed to defeat the Goblin King?'

'Maybe five minutes with the sword and he'll throw himself off a cliff or something,' said

Raven Boy. Elf Girl didn't look convinced.

> *'I love the summer, I love the spring,*
> *When autumn comes it's just the thing,*
> *And I even love the winter too,*
> *As long as I can be in love with you.'*

'And why,' said Raven Boy, 'does it only sing cheesy love songs?'

Elf Girl pulled a face as if she might be sick.

People were coming and going in the street, and occasionally they would stop and stare at the scruffy bird boy, a girl with pointy ears and pointy-toed boots, a sword that sang really badly and a dancing rat.

'I can't stand it,' said Elf Girl, and then someone threw something at them. It was a coin, and it rolled up to Elf Girl's pointy-toed boots.

'If I pay you enough, will you go away?' shouted a voice from the crowd, and everyone laughed. Before they knew what was happening, a dozen more coins clanged onto the paving stones where they stood.

'Come on,' said Raven Boy. 'Let's take the money and clear off before they realise we can't make it stop.'

He scurried around, picking up the money.

'Where shall we go?' asked Elf Girl. 'We're supposed to wait for the Mayor.'

'Never mind him,' said Raven Boy. 'Let's head to the castle and go and see Lord Socket ourselves.'

Although they couldn't see the castle, they knew from their flying carpet ride that it was built on a hill high above the town.

They headed into the maze of streets and alleys, and were soon lost. All they could do was keep heading up, turning this way and that, attracting puzzled stares from passers-by as the sword kept up its endless stream of terrible tunes.

'Hey baby, you're the one for me,
I'm the luckiest guy around,
Come over here and you will see,
The wonderful love that I have found.'

'I am going to kill myself,' said Elf Girl. 'Or someone. If it doesn't stop singing soon.'

Raven Boy checked Elf Girl's ears for signs that they were turning red. They seemed okay but he was worried nonetheless.

'I'm not sure it will ever stop,' he said.

'Never? Never?' cried Elf Girl. 'That's impossible.'

Raven Boy didn't answer.

Elf Girl stared at him.

'Isn't it?' she said in a small voice. 'Maybe we could forget saving the world. Save our eardrums instead.'

'No!' said Raven Boy, fiercely. 'Don't you remember what the Goblin King is doing to our forest? Don't you remember all the bad things we've seen? The curse on Terror Town is just the latest. We have to go on, we can't give up now! We have the sword and very soon we'll find the tears and . . .'

'Yes!' yelled Elf Girl. 'Yes, okay! I get it. I remember. Lecture over. Just do one thing for me?'

'What?'

'You carry the flipping sword for a bit.'

Raven Boy gulped. He nodded and held out his hand for Elf Girl to pass him the sword, and the moment he took it from her, it stopped singing! Just like that. Halfway through a lovely number about skipping through the meadows, hand in hand.

Rat gave a sad squeak.

Elf Girl said, 'Thank hedgehogs for that.'

Raven Boy said, 'Well, that's odd.'

They both stared at the silent sword, and then Elf Girl said, 'He hasn't even got hands.'

TEN

When Elf Girl gets home, the first thing she's going to do is wash her hair. Three times.

It wasn't long before they found the castle.

It was big. In fact, it would be more accurate to say it was very big, the kind of very big that is pretty much the same as enormous.

They stood in front of the enormous front gates to the enormous castle, and felt very small indeed. The kind of very small that is pretty much the same as tiny.

'Er, maybe we should wait for the Mayor,' said Raven Boy.

'Um,' said Elf Girl. 'Yes. Maybe we should.'

Rat squeaked loudly because he was grumpy that the nice music had stopped, but also because it seemed to him that the pointy girl and the bird boy were about to chicken out, just when they seemed to be getting somewhere.

'He's right,' said Raven Boy. 'He said . . .'

'Yes, I get it. He thinks we ought to get on with it.'

'Uh-huh,' said Raven Boy. 'That's right! Are you learning rat language now?'

Elf Girl sighed and wondered for the fortieth time whether Raven Boy had been made any less dim-witted by the wish she'd made in the desert.

She reached for an enormous door knocker that made her feel even tinier, because it was so heavy to lift, and when she let it bash back down on the door, the sound was like a clap of thunder echoing around the mountains.

Way, way above their heads, a shutter opened and someone stuck their head out. He

looked down and saw a girl with a bow and
a boy with a sword and without thinking any
more about it, pulled a lever in the wall.

At that exact moment, the paving stones
on which Elf Girl and Raven Boy were standing
swung open like a trapdoor, and they hurtled
down a long, dark chute, tumbling head-over-
heels, screaming at the tops of their voices.

The chute seemed to go on forever, and
just when they thought it would never stop, it did.

They bumped onto a cold hard floor somewhere that was completely dark, and next second heard a familiar sound. Of singing.

'If you're the one for me-ee-ee,
How happy I would be-ee-ee,
And I'm the one for yo-oo-ou,
How happy you are too-oo-oo.'

'Oh! Oh, no!' wailed Elf Girl. 'Not again.'

'I'm sorry!' cried Raven Boy. 'I dropped it when we landed!'

'Quick! Quick, find it! Please find it!'

They scrabbled about in the dark, until finally Elf Girl put her hand on the sword.

'I've got it!' she cried, but the sword was still singing. 'Come here, Raven Boy! Let me give it to you.'

'One little buttercup, said to another cup,
How much do I love you?
The other little buttercup said to the other cup,
As much as I love you too.'

'Oh, monkey-face! No, please!' wailed Elf Girl again. 'Where are you, Raven Boy?'

'Be careful!' said Raven Boy, unhappy at the thought of Elf Girl waving a sword at him in the total darkness, even if it was one that only sang soppy love songs.

'Here!' she said. 'I'm pointing the blunt end at you.'

She never had time to give it back to Raven Boy, because suddenly they were blinded by bright light flooding into the room.

They felt themselves shoved about a bit, and next second they heard a door slide shut and were plunged into darkness once more, at which point they noticed two things.

'My bow's gone!' yelled Elf Girl.

'They've taken the sword, too! Haven't you noticed how quiet it is?'

Elf Girl listened for a moment.

'Ah,' she said. 'Oh, that's bliss . . . But they've still taken my bow! How dare they! I'll cut them up into little pieces!'

'With what?' asked Raven Boy. 'They've taken the sword.'

'Oh, yes,' said Elf Girl. She was quiet, and Raven Boy heard her shifting about in the darkness. Then she said, 'Raven Boy, it's very dark in here.'

'I know. Rat, are you there?'

Rat squeaked.

'Oh, good,' said Raven Boy.

'Now what do we do?' asked Elf Girl.

'I don't know,' said Raven Boy. 'I suppose we wait until they come back for us.'

Elf Girl thought about this for a long time.

Then she said, 'But supposing they never do?'

They found each other in the dark, all three of them, and though they didn't say anything out loud, they were very gloomy, thinking of how many times they'd been locked up, or trapped, on their adventures so far. Somehow, being locked in the dark with no explanation seemed to be the very worst thing, and all Raven Boy could think was, supposing Elf Girl is right. Supposing they never come back? Ever?

But they did come back.

Many, many hours went by, and then the door slid open again, only now it wasn't so bright outside. Hands grabbed them and dragged them out. Rat scampered into Raven Boy's pocket for safety, and they gasped as they were led through many long, posh corridors, up stairways, and along winding passages, deep into the heart of Lord Socket's castle.

Eventually, they came to a gigantic throne room, at the far end of which they saw a group of people, among them the Mayor, and someone, a tall young man who they guessed had to be Lord Socket, sitting on the largest chair they'd ever seen.

They were forced to kneel in front of Lord Socket. The Mayor stared at them, saying nothing.

Raven Boy was about to open his mouth and beg for his life when Lord Socket stood up suddenly and said, 'Please, please, please make it shut up!'

For a second they didn't understand what he meant, but then they heard the sound of singing coming from a room somewhere behind the throne, and Elf Girl and Raven Boy risked a smile.

> *'Don't you know how I love you?*
> *Me, o my, I love you true.*
> *I love you truly true,*
> *A-shooby-dooby-dooby-doo.'*

Eleven

**Rat thinks the sword's singing
is the best he's ever heard. But
then again, he'd never heard
any music before he left home
with Raven Boy and Elf Girl.**

Raven Boy and Elf Girl looked around them.

As they did, the sound of dreadful singing still wafted into the room, and they became
aware that Lord Socket was staring at them.

'Well?' he said.

'Well, what?' snapped Elf Girl, who was
getting fed up at being spoken to so rudely by
almost everyone they met.

'She means hello,' explained Raven Boy. 'And so do I. I'm Raven Boy and this is Elf Girl.'

Socket looked at them both, his eyes narrowing.

'Are those your real names?' he said. 'They sound like the aliases of naughty criminals to me!'

'Naughty?' cried Elf Girl.

'Crinimals?' cried Raven Boy.

Elf Girl sighed.

'Cri-mi-nals,' she spelled out. 'No, they are not our real names but they're all you're getting from us.'

'Elf Girl!' hissed Raven Boy. 'Be careful!'

'Never mind your silly names,' said Lord Socket. 'Why were you attacking my castle?'

'We're not!' said Raven Boy. 'We came to speak to you, that's all. He can tell you that.'

Raven Boy pointed at the Mayor.

Socket ignored this and waved his hand to a guard, who flung open a door, through which they saw the sword lying on a table. Socket led the way and two more guards pulled Elf Girl and Raven Boy into the room.

'Hey! That's my bow!'

Elf Girl made towards her bow, which lay next to the sword, but the guards grabbed her straight away.

Socket pointed at Raven Boy.

'Make the sword stop singing, or else!'

Raven Boy sighed.

'I may as well,' he said to Elf Girl. 'It's starting to drive me nuts.'

'And no funny business,' warned Socket. 'One wrong move with that sword and I'll drop you from the highest battlements in the castle.'

'Don't worry, he barely knows one end from the other,' said Elf Girl.

'Thanks, Elf Girl,' said Raven Boy. 'Let's not give all our secrets away, eh?'

'When you've quite finished!' roared Socket. 'Will you please make the sword shut up!'

'I'm gonna love you forever . . .' the sword was singing, meanwhile.

'. . . Forever, because that's so clever,
I'm gonna love you like a dog,
Like a fire loves a log.'

Rat popped his head out of Raven Boy's pocket and was bopping about.

'Please make it shut up! Now!' wailed

Socket, losing his cool.

Raven Boy sauntered over to the table and picked up the sword. It stopped singing straight away.

Socket stepped forward and grabbed the sword from him.

'If you love me true,
I'll love you too,' sang the sword.

Socket shrieked and chucked it back at Raven Boy, who caught it without managing to slice his fingers off.

'No wonder it was left at the top of that tree in the middle of the desert,' said Raven Boy to Elf Girl.

'It's starting to make sense,' she agreed.

'Show me how to do that,' said Socket.

'I can't,' said Raven Boy.

'Why not?' asked Socket.

'Because I don't know how I do it. It's just quiet when I hold it, but not when Elf Girl does. Or you.'

'Or anyone else!'

The new voice belonged to a strange-looking man who had entered the room. He was dressed from head to foot in a long gown with stars sewn all over it. The hood was pulled back to reveal a face so old that even the wrinkles had wrinkles. He had a long beard that reached halfway down his front but strangely almost no hair on his head. Despite his age he seemed full of energy as he pointed his finger towards Raven Boy.

'Anyone but the wise fool!' he declared.

'The what?' asked Elf Girl.

'How rude!' said Raven Boy.

'Listen to me, bird boy,' snapped Socket.
'Either tell me how your magical sword works
or I won't be very happy, got it?'

'Er, right,' said Raven Boy. 'Believe me,
I'd love to tell you how, but we only got the
thing about half an hour before you locked us
in that dark dungeon. Elf Girl's right, I don't
know one end of a sword from the other and I
certainly don't know how to make it stop singing.
It just does when I pick it up.'

'And anyway,' said Elf Girl. 'We weren't attacking your castle. We were coming to speak to you about finding some things of ours that were stolen because we need them to help us defeat the Goblin King. He can tell you!'

She pointed at the Mayor, who had been strangely quiet all this time.

'Tell him!' said Elf Girl, but the Mayor raised his eyebrows as if he didn't know what she was talking about.

The funny man with stars on his robe stepped closer to Raven Boy, inspecting him.

Then suddenly, he threw both arms out wide and his eyes glazed over. He began to mumble, over and over and louder and louder.

> *'The wise fool comes from far away,*
> *He has a sword that can sing,*
> *He knows no fear, and will defeat*
> *The evil Goblin King.'*

'Oh no,' moaned Lord Socket. 'Klingsor's off again . . . '

Klingsor didn't seem to hear anything, or

see anyone, but kept repeating his strange verse.

'Klingsor!' yelled Socket right in his ear. 'Time for your lie-down!'

Klingsor's eyes popped open, he pointed at Raven Boy, and then fell backwards on the carpet in a dead faint.

Elf Girl stared at Klingsor, then at Raven Boy.

'EEEP!' said Raven Boy.

TWELVE

What Raven Boy and Elf Girl don't know is that Klingsor has never been wrong about a prophecy, ever. Well, apart from the time he told Lord Socket his feet would fall off the following day.

There was silence in the room for a good long while, until people started whispering and then the whispering became a muttering and then the muttering became a hullabaloo.

And what they were all saying was this: 'Klingsor! Klingsor has seen something. A prophecy! A prophecy!'

This went on for some time until finally

Lord Socket stamped his foot.

'Be quiet!' he yelled. 'Silence! I will have silence in my court!'

Finally he got everyone to stop talking, but they were still staring at Raven Boy.

Stepping over Klingsor, Socket walked towards him.

'Who are you?' he asked. 'And what is your real name?'

'Even I don't know his real name!' shouted Elf Girl. 'And I'm his best friend!'

'You are?' said Raven Boy. He looked surprised, but he was smiling.

Rat squeaked.

'You're both my best friends,' Raven Boy said.

'How sweet!' snarled Lord Socket. 'But let me get back to the question of who you are and what you are doing in my castle!'

'We came to speak to you,' said Elf Girl, in a slow voice that showed she was getting cross, 'because the Mayor told us you're in charge of Terror Town. We have lost two very important things, namely a bottle of oasis water and a stroppy carpet. If we do not find them, then we will not be able to save the world from the Goblin King, which is something you ought to want us to do since your town is being attacked by his forces every night!'

By the end of her speech, Elf Girl was yelling and her ears were red hot.

There was stunned silence in the court and Socket stared back at Elf Girl, a strange expression on his face. He blinked and said, 'The Goblin King?'

'Yes, the Goblin King! We're here to defeat him and at the very least you ought to help us.'

Socket waved his finger at her.

'You don't know what it's like!' he said. 'Every night! Nasty things attacking the town. We shut the town gates at dusk but somehow these monsters keep getting in!'

'You seem pretty safe up here in your castle!' said Raven Boy.

'Oh yes, we are,' said Socket. 'And I intend to keep it that way.'

'But what about the rest of your people? The ones who don't live in the castle? They're being terrorised every night!'

'Too bad. If you think I'm stupid enough to risk my safety on that lot out there, you're mistaken.'

Elf Girl stamped her foot.

'You! You coward!'

Socket didn't even bat an eyelid at this insult.

'Now,' he said, 'for the final time. Tell me how to keep the sword quiet, and tell me how this magical bow of yours works, or I will throw you out of the castle. And night is about to fall.'

'You wouldn't!' declared Elf Girl. 'You wouldn't dare! Even you couldn't be that cowardly and mean!'

Two minutes later, Elf Girl and Raven Boy sat on the back doorstep of the castle.

'Elf Girl . . .' began Raven Boy.

'Don't say anything,' she said, grumpily. 'I know. Me and my big mouth.'

'I wasn't going to say that,' said Raven Boy.

'No? What then?'

'Two things. First thing, I like what you said about being friends.'

Elf Girl looked shy, which was most unlike her.

'Oh,' she said. 'I meant it.'

'Thank you,' said Raven Boy. 'I never had a best friend before. Of course, I had my animal friends, but I never had a best friend. Not one who can talk.'

'But you can talk to the animals, can't you?'

'Yes,' said Raven Boy. 'But it's not like we talk about that much. Where the best nuts are, whether it's going to rain. That's more or less it. What a big meany that Socket is, though. Throwing us out of the castle!'

'I know! Such a shame too.'

'A shame? Why?'

'He was terribly handsome,' said Elf Girl.

Raven Boy went quiet then. He didn't like that thought much.

'Anyway,' said Elf Girl. 'What was the second thing?'

Raven Boy still felt sulky, but the second thing was too important not to mention.

'Where are we going to sleep?' he said. 'It will be dark soon, and then . . .'

'Anything could happen. Raven Boy, you're right. We need to find somewhere, and quickly. We could go back to the hotel. Terrible Tim's has to be better than zombies or whatever's coming tonight.'

'Agreed!' said Raven Boy, and they were about to set off, when they saw another door open in the castle wall.

'Look!' whispered Raven Boy, grabbing Elf Girl's arm. 'Look!'

It was the Mayor. He crept out of the castle, looking about him as if he didn't want to be seen. When he thought he was safe, he hurried away into the streets, heading not towards his own house, but in another direction entirely.

'What's he up to?' wondered Elf Girl.

'I think we ought to find out,' said Raven Boy. 'Come on!'

'The sun's setting!' whispered Elf Girl as they hurried along. 'We need to hide. Soon!'

'Just a little further,' said Raven Boy. 'I want to know what he's doing. Something's not right.'

They soon found out what that something was.

Just as the sun set, they saw the Mayor reach the gates of the town, which were locked and barred, shut tight to keep out the Goblin King's monsters.

The Mayor took a last look around, and then he lifted the bars, unlocked the locks, and opened the gates.

'It's him!' hissed Elf Girl. 'He's been unlocking the gates every night!'

'Never mind that,' cried Raven Boy. 'Look! Werewolves! Run!'

THIRTEEN

**Unlike zombies, werewolves
are very fussy about what
they eat. They like humans;
and running humans are best,
since they're all warmed up
when they eat them.**

It is entirely possible that Elf Girl and Raven
Boy had never run so fast in their lives.

They sprinted through Terror Town,
without thinking where they were going. A
large silver moon shone down, giving them
more than enough light to see the danger they
were in.

Behind them, they could hear the pounding

paws of the half-wolves, half-men who seemed
desperate to sink their teeth into the delicate
backsides of Raven Boy and Elf Girl.

Rat had visions of being swallowed
whole and had hidden in the deepest of Raven
Boy's many pockets, and all the while there was
a dreadful howl which chilled the blood just to
hear it.

'This way!' screeched Raven Boy, and
tugged Elf Girl into an alleyway. But the
werewolves could smell them as easily as see
them, and hurtled after them.

'I can't run much further!' screamed Elf
Girl, but somehow she managed to keep going.

As they ran they could hear the werewolves

charging at people's doors. Some were strong, but others gave way and they heard screams as people burst out of their back doors, to join Elf Girl and Raven Boy in running madly through Terror Town.

'Over there!' panted Raven Boy, spotting the smallest alley they'd seen so far.

But they emerged into a square, only to find that there was no way out. A dead end.

'**EEP!**' cheeped Raven Boy.

'Oh no!' wailed Elf Girl. 'Trapped like rats!'

An angry muffled squeak came from Raven Boy's pocket.

They spun around in time to see three werewolves stalk into the square. Seeing that they had their prey trapped, the beasts slowed to a walk. They had been running on four paws, but now they stood up, and towered over the shivering wrecks that were Elf Girl and Raven Boy.

The terrified twosome edged towards each other, feeling for each other's hands.

'I don't want to be eaten,' said Raven Boy. 'We've come so far.'

'Yes,' agreed Elf Girl. 'It's enough to make you seriously think about being vegetarian.'

Then she fainted, and Raven Boy could think of nothing better to do than to join her.

Unfortunately for them, they woke up again straight away.

'They might have eaten us while we were out cold!' muttered Raven Boy, as the biggest of the three creatures took a step closer.

Raven Boy shut his eyes, and held Elf Girl's hand even tighter and then he heard a voice he recognised.

'Oi! No you don't!'

Raven Boy opened his eyes to see where the voice had come from. Then, from a rooftop behind them, someone, or something, jumped into the square onto the nearest wolf, who was squashed flat.

It was Cedric, the largest, and, to be honest, smelliest of the three trolls who'd been following them ever since they'd left Fright Forest.

'Oh my goodness!' said Elf Girl.

There was another thump, and another, and the other two trolls, Bob and Bert, jumped from the roof too, neatly flattening the two remaining werewolves.

'Take that!' roared Bob.

'Hairy monster!' laughed Bert.

Cedric turned round and faced Elf Girl
and Raven Boy, who didn't know whether to be
delighted or terrified.

'Er,' said Raven Boy. 'Thank you. I think.'

'No one eats our dinner!' said Cedric.
Then he laughed in a most unpleasant way.

'Oh,' said Elf Girl. 'I was rather hoping
you might have given up on the idea of us being
dinner.'

'Or lunch,' added Raven Boy.

'Or breakfast or anything,' finished Elf Girl.

'Sorry,' chuckled Cedric. 'No such luck. Now then boys, who shall we eat first?'

Bob and Bert began to have a discussion about who it would be better to sink their rotten teeth into first, until Cedric gave them both a slap round their grubby, hairy ears.

'Shut up!' he cried. 'Honestly! You two do my noggin. You really do.'

'Sorry, Cedric,' said Bob.

'Sorry, Cedric,' said Bert.

'Sorry, Cedric,' said Raven Boy. 'But could I ask something?'

'The dinner is talking,' said Bert.

'I still say it's more like breakfast-time than dinner,' said Bob.

'Excuse me?' said Raven Boy.

'What?' Cedric asked.

'Well, it's just that I would like you to let us go.'

Cedric roared with laughter.

'Let you go? Let you go! Ha! That's funny.'

'You have to! Or else the Goblin King

will take over the whole world!'

Cedric stopped laughing.

'Goblin King?' he said.

'Yes!' said Raven Boy. 'We're going to find him. And defeat him. Stop him destroying everything.'

Cedric looked at Bob and Bert.

'You must have heard of the Goblin King!' said Elf Girl. 'Haven't you? He's going to destroy everything unless we stop him! Including you!'

'So you have to let us go!' said Raven Boy.

'Yes,' said Cedric. 'We've heard of the Goblin King. Yes, we have.'

Bob and Bert nodded.

'You're going to find him?' Cedric asked.

'We just said so, didn't we?' said Elf Girl, crossly.

Raven Boy nudged her in the ribs.

'Shh,' he said. He turned to Cedric. 'Yes, we're going to find him, and put a stop to his naughty behaviour.'

Cedric waved a big clumsy hand at Raven Boy.

'How? How are you going to stop him? No one can defeat him.'

'We can!' said Raven Boy. 'We have magical things. The Tears of the Moon and the Singing Sword. We've been told they can defeat him. Only we don't have them any more.'

Cedric seemed to be thinking hard and it caused him great pain to do so.

'Where are they then?'

'Somewhere in this town!' said Raven Boy. 'The sword is in Lord Socket's castle. Someone stole the tears but they can't be far away.'

'And then you're going to defeat the Goblin King?'

'Yes!' cried Elf Girl. Then she added, in a quiet voice, 'Only we don't know where he is.'

'Oh, that's easy,' said Bob. 'Everyone knows he lives in the Creepy Caves.'

Raven Boy looked at Elf Girl.

'Well, it was never going to be Cosy Caves, was it?'

Cedric looked in even more pain as he spoke very slowly to Raven Boy and Elf Girl.

'I am thinking,' he said. 'I am thinking this: we will make a deal.'

'A deal?' asked Raven Boy.

'Yes, a deal. The deal is this; we will promise not to eat you . . .'

'We will?' wailed Bert.

'Shh! We will promise not to eat you, and we will take you to the Creepy Caves, if you defeat the Goblin King.'

Raven Boy was speechless.

'You will? You'll promise not to eat us?'

'Yeah,' said Cedric. 'At least, not until after the Goblin King's all done for.'

'What?' cried Elf Girl.

'Deal?' asked Cedric.

'Deal!' said Raven Boy, at which point Elf Girl shrieked 'No!'

But it was too late, the deal was done.

Fourteen

**Elf Girl thinks that Raven Boy is
very stupid indeed to trust the trolls
with their lives. She's almost
certainly right about this.**

'Why did you agree to that?' said Elf Girl.

'As long as the Goblin King is dead,' said
Raven Boy, 'it doesn't matter about us.'

'Yes it does!' said Elf Girl and even Rat
squeaked in agreement.

'Anyway,' said Raven Boy, ignoring them
both. 'I have a feeling that by the time we've
travelled to the Creepy Caves together we'll be such

friends that they would never dream of eating us.'

Bob nudged Bert in the ribs.

'What a dream! Eatin' 'em! Eh?'

Bert chuckled a dirty laugh.

Elf Girl groaned.

'Raven Boy, you are the most . . .'

She never finished what she was saying,
because just then half a dozen werewolves
burst into the square, with slobbering chops
and terrifying teeth.

Elf Girl screamed and Raven Boy shrieked,
but before they knew what was happening,
Cedric, Bob and Bert laid into the furry fiends
like a terrifying whirlwind.

Two were biffed on the head before they'd even taken another step, a third got a boot up its behind so hard that it was knocked right out of the square and onto the rooftops, and the final three ran away squealing with teeth marks in their fur.

'Nice work, boys,' said Cedric, pulling some wolf fur out of his teeth.

Raven Boy turned to Elf Girl.

'See?' he said. 'Not such a bad deal, after all, is it?'

Elf Girl wasn't convinced.

'Mr Troll?' she asked.

Cedric turned and smiled down at her.

'Yes, my dear little fing, what is it? Oh, and do call me Cedric.'

'Er, right,' she said. 'Cedric. You promise not to eat us?'

'We does.'

'Why? Why do you want to go to the Goblin King? I can't believe you're suddenly interested in saving the world.'

'Ah!' said Cedric. 'And you'd be right. We're not. But as it happens, the Goblin King has something we want.'

'What?'

'That's our little secret, isn't it? Only we want this thing, and we can't kill him ourselves. He's too strong, see? But if you know how to, then that's a whole other kind of fish, innit?'

'I see,' said Elf Girl. 'I think.'

Raven Boy nodded.

'Well, that's fine,' he said. 'But you have to help us. We have to get the Singing Sword back. And find the Tears of the Moon.'

'Agreed,' said Cedric.

'And you have to promise not to eat us. Or anyone else we say not to eat.'

'Agreed,' said Cedric. 'At least, until the Goblin King is dead, right?'

Raven Boy's smile faltered.

'Right,' he said.

Elf Girl slapped her forehead.

'Bird brain!' she said.

'Is that your name?' asked Cedric.

'No, of course not,' said Raven Boy. 'My name is Raven Boy. I told you that before. When we were all locked up by that crazy wizard in the Monster Mountains.'

'Did you?' asked Cedric. He turned to his friends. 'Did he?'

They nodded.

'And this is Elf Girl, and Rat,' said Raven Boy, smiling. 'Now, the first thing to do is to get back into the castle, and get the Singing Sword.'

'Singing Sword?' asked Cedric. 'Whassat?'

'Oh, you're going to love it,' said Elf Girl in a way that sounded as if she didn't mean it at all.

'The castle?' said Cedric. 'So we need to get rid of these doggy things first, right?'

Bob and Bert chuckled again.

'Doggy things?' asked Raven Boy. 'You mean the werewolves?'

But Cedric, Bob and Bert weren't listening.

They were already striding out of the square and back towards the werewolf-filled streets of Terror Town.

'Come on, boys!' cried Cedric. 'It's wolf-munching time!'

Elf Girl stared at Raven Boy.

'Are you sure this is a good idea?' she asked.

'Come on! We don't want to get left behind.'

'We don't?'

'We don't. We'll be safer with them on our side.'

Elf Girl knew that was true, for now. But how long could they trust the trolls not to get peckish and forget about the deal they'd made with Raven Boy?

Fifteen

The stories that Raven Boy and Elf Girl keep hearing about the Goblin King get worse all the time. And they still don't know how the Singing Sword or the Tears of the Moon are supposed to defeat him.

Raven Boy and Elf Girl followed the trolls, who were having a merry old time clobbering werewolves and occasionally nibbling one when they felt hungry.

'Are you sure this is a good idea?' asked Elf Girl as they ran.

'Totally,' said Raven Boy. 'We'd have been chewed by wolves by now if it wasn't for these three.'

As they made their way through the town towards the castle, they had to keep half an eye on Cedric, Bob and Bert, who were keen to nibble some of the townspeople too.

'You're not to eat anyone in this town!' said Elf Girl sternly.

'Awww,' moaned Bert. 'Do we have to do what she says?'

'Yeah, we does,' said Cedric. 'We made an agreement, right?'

Bob moaned too, but Cedric bashed him on the top of his head to keep him quiet.

'Goblin King, remember?' he said, and that was enough to get Bob back to work fighting the werewolves.

'This is all very strange,' said Raven Boy.

'What?' asked Elf Girl.

'If I had told you that we'd be saved from man-eating werewolves by werewolf-eating trolls a few weeks ago, you wouldn't have believed me.'

Elf Girl nodded.

'That's not the only strange thing though, is it?'

'What do you mean?' asked Raven Boy, skipping over an unconscious werewolf.

'That business in the castle earlier on. That strange man with the strange name. Klingsor, was it?'

'I think so,' said Raven Boy. 'Yes, I've been wondering about that too. What does prophecy mean?'

'Can't your new super-smart brain tell you that?'

'It can, only it doesn't want to just now.'

'A prophecy is when someone tells you

about the future.'

'Before it's happened?'

'Well obviously, or it wouldn't be the future any more, would it?'

'I think he was a wizard,' said Raven Boy. 'Did you see the way he was dressed? He reminded me of Jeremy in the Monster Mountains. And his friend, Simon.'

'Of course he was a wizard, but what about that thing he said? That rhyme?'

'I've forgotten it,' said Raven Boy.

'No, you haven't,' said Elf Girl. 'You're just pretending. Anyway, I can remember:

"The wise fool comes from far away,
He has a sword that can sing,
He knows no fear, and will defeat
The evil Goblin King."'

'Thanks for reminding me,' said Raven Boy. 'Anyway, it doesn't make sense. Who's the wise fool? What does that even mean?'

'It means you, dummy,' said Elf Girl.

But Raven Boy wasn't sure, and shaking

his head, he sped up a little as the trolls were
nearly at the castle.

A lot of the townspeople had joined them,
realising the trolls were on their side and
protecting them from the monsters.

Soon, the crowd had grown massive, and
it arrived at the castle gates. The werewolves
were nowhere to be seen. It looked like the
trolls had defeated them all.

Cedric, Bob and Bert forced their way to the front of the crowd and began to slap their big hands on the doors.

'Look out!' warned Raven Boy. 'There's a trapdoor under your feet . . .'

Too late!

With a loud yell, all three trolls dropped out of sight down the long dark chute, just as Raven Boy and Elf Girl had done.

The cheering crowd went quiet.

From far below, they heard the sound of three thumps.

Then there was silence, followed by an enormous crash, which sounded exactly like three trolls breaking down a large wooden door. From inside the castle, Raven Boy and Elf Girl heard crashes, screams, thuds and yells, until finally, with a deafening thump, the gates in front of them opened and a drawbridge fell down over the trapdoor.

Cedric stuck his head out.

'Come inside,' he said. 'And quickly, from the looks of things.'

He nodded with his chin, to behind the

crowd, where a pack of werewolves were charging towards them at top speed.

Raven Boy screamed, which started everyone screaming and stampeding inside the castle.

'Close the gates, close the gates!' wailed Elf Girl as the last of the townspeople made it inside.

Bob and Bert swung the gates shut, and they heard wolves clawing at the wood outside.

'Do you think they can get in?' asked Elf Girl.

'I hope not!' said Raven Boy. 'It just has to hold until dawn, I suppose.'

'Yes, you're right,' cried Elf Girl, 'and that reminds me. In the meantime, we can tell Socket how the beasts are getting into his town every night!'

'Yes! The Mayor! That rotten cheater!'

'I can think of worse things to say,' said Elf Girl.

'Yes, well, that's why I'm nicer than you,' said Raven Boy, and they led the way into the castle, with the trolls bashing any guards who tried to stop them, and the good people of Terror Town following behind, ooh-ing and aah-ing at the magnificent decorations.

SIXTEEN

It's true; trolls smell very bad.
But that's only because they've
never heard of washing or
tooth-brushing.

They must have looked a sight when they
barged into the throne room, because Lord
Socket had an expression on his face as if he'd
just swallowed a grandfather clock.

'How dare you!' he yelled, but the people
of Terror Town were in no mood to listen.

'How dare *you*!' they roared.

'You abandoned us!'

'Left us to the mercy of monsters every night!'

Lord Socket tried to put up a good fight, but it was no use. In moments all his guards were overpowered and when Bert the troll sat on his throne and promptly broke it, Lord Socket burst into tears like a small girl.

'This is *my* castle,' he wailed.

'Not any more, it isn't!' said someone, and then they explained how they were going to move in because it was safer than the town.

'Anyway,' said Elf Girl, standing with her hands on her hips in front of the snivelling Socket. 'We know how the beasties are getting in, the zombies and whatnot.'

Socket looked at her.

'You do?' he asked, miserably.

'Yes, we do. And stop being such a cry-baby. It's not so handsome.'

Socket wiped his nose.

'What's been going on?'

'It's the Mayor,' explained Raven Boy. 'He's opening the gates every night.'

'The Mayor? Ridiculous!'

'We saw him!' said Elf Girl. 'With our own eyes. He let these werewolves in tonight.'

'He did? You saw him?' asked Socket.

'We did, with our own eyes. You ought to have a word with him.'

'A word?' roared Socket, sounding more like his usual bossy self. 'I'll have his head off!'

'You'll have to find him first,' said Raven Boy. 'It looks like the whole town is here, but him.'

'But why would he let these beasties in every night? And why isn't he scared of being eaten himself?' asked Elf Girl.

'Unless he's in league with the Goblin King!' said Raven Boy, and there was the sound of the penny dropping in everyone's heads.

'Why!' cried Socket. 'That fiend! I'll have his head off twice!'

'Oi!' said Bert, who was standing by a window, looking down at the streets below the castle.

'What?' asked Cedric.

'I fink you ought to have a look down 'ere,' said Bert.

'Not now,' said Cedric.

'Well, I dunno,' said Bert. 'But you might wanna see what's going on down 'ere.'

What he'd seen turned out to be really quite frightening.

There was a new werewolf in the street. The strongest, tallest one they'd seen. It was taller than Cedric, the largest troll, and looked super-mean and hungry.

The wolf began to jump at the gates, pounding them and falling back.

'It's like the King Wolf,' said Bob. 'It's

gonna eat us all.'

'It will have to get in here first!'

With a mighty crash, the werewolf leaped, splintering the gates into a thousand pieces.

They heard it howl, and Raven Boy and Elf Girl were treated to the sight of the three scary trolls, who'd been hunting them for days, turn scared themselves.

'That can't be good,' said Raven Boy, swallowing nervously. 'Cedric, you can beat this big dog, can't you?'

Cedric looked at Raven Boy.

'Are you joking? Have you seen the size of him?'

'So what do we do?' asked Elf Girl.

'Run!' shouted Cedric.

'And cry!' yelled Bob, as the giant werewolf bounded into the throne room, and slid to a stop, spoilt for choice as to who to eat first.

Everyone began to scream, but Raven Boy and Elf Girl didn't.

'Come on!' shouted Elf Girl. 'We have to try!'

She dived behind the throne and threw open the doors to the room where they'd last seen her bow and the Singing Sword.

'I'm gonna love you like a banana,' sang the sword.

'Still here, then,' muttered Elf Girl, and grabbed her bow, while Raven Boy snatched up the sword.

'How was it going to rhyme "banana"?' said Raven Boy, running back into the throne room after Elf Girl, who had already drawn her bow and was firing at the giant werewolf.

She fired again and again, but sadly all she was shooting at the wolf was useless things: a nice pot plant, in its pot, a jelly, not in its mould, a startled weasel, a book about bee-keeping.

The wolf seemed amused, then irritated, and was about to leap at Elf Girl, when Klingsor stepped forward and whispered in Elf Girl's ear.

Her very next shot was a fireball the size of a baby elephant. It hit the wolf, who caught fire, and began to scrabble around howling terribly.

Raven Boy cheered as the wolf threw itself out of the open window into the streets far below.

Everyone rushed to the window amazed to see the wolf alive but bounding out of the town with its tail still smouldering.

'You did it!' cried Raven Boy happily. 'You did it!'

'Yay!' shouted Cedric, Bob and Bert as one.

Elf Girl stood looking bemused. She turned to Klingsor.

'You did it,' she said. 'Not me.'

'No,' said Klingsor. 'You did it yourself. All I did was make a suggestion about how to use the bow a little more, well, usefully.'

'Wow!' said Raven Boy. 'He told you the secret of how to use it. Properly I mean. What was it?'

'Ah!' said Klingsor. 'Shh, my girl. It wouldn't be a secret then, would it? She knows how to use the bow now, and that's all that matters.'

'Oh,' said Raven Boy. 'That's so annoying. But yes, I guess as long as she knows what she's doing.'

'And you,' said Klingsor. 'Do you know what you're doing, my wise fool?'

'Why are you calling me that?' asked Raven Boy.

'Because you are the wise fool, are you not?' said Klingsor.

'That's so rude!' said Raven Boy grumpily.

'Not at all!' said Klingsor. 'You are the hero who will save us all.'

'I am?' asked Raven Boy.

And that made Klingsor tell his little rhyme again,

> *'The wise fool comes from far away,*
> *He has a sword that can sing,*
> *He knows no fear, and will defeat*
> *The evil Goblin King.'*

'Knows no fear?' wailed Raven Boy. 'I'm terrified!'

'Be that as it may,' said Klingsor, 'you are the only one for whom the sword will be quiet. You are its rightful owner, it appears. And you will save us from the Goblin King!'

'I will?' said Raven Boy, and then, because it had been at least half an hour since the last time, he said 'EEP!' once, and fainted on the carpet.

SEVENTEEN

One night, Raven Boy had a dream about the Goblin King. It was so scary that when he woke up his teeth were still chattering.

Raven Boy woke to feel something licking his nose.

'Eww!' he said, then saw it was Rat and sat up.

'Oh,' he said, because he was surrounded by everyone in Terror Town, from Lord Socket to the smallest child. They were all staring at him.

'So!' said Lord Socket. 'Your friend with

the pointy ears has told us about your mission to defeat the Goblin King.'

'She has?' asked Raven Boy.

Elf Girl nodded enthusiastically.

'She has,' said Socket. 'And Klingsor has told us of the prophecy of the wise fool, who will save us from the evil of the Goblin King.'

'He did?' asked Raven Boy.

'He did,' said Socket. 'And I have declared to the people that you are now in charge of the official war party to go and fight the Goblin King.'

'You said that?'

'I said that,' said Socket.

'And no fainting,' said Elf Girl. 'That's not going to help anyone.'

'It might help me,' said Raven Boy. 'If I faint I won't have to listen to this nonsense.'

'That's enough of that!' said Socket. 'You are in charge. I will help you in any way I can.'

'Any way? Like letting me go home?'

'Any way except that.'

Raven Boy sighed. He stared at everyone for a long time, and then he stood up.

'Okay then,' he said. It wasn't the most
impressive speech of all time, but everyone cheered.

'What shall we do first?' asked Cedric.

'That's easy,' said Raven Boy. 'First, we have to find the Tears of the Moon, and our magic carpet.'

'How do we do that?' asked Bob.

'That's easy too. We have the whole town here, more or less. Since the town is now free from werewolves, everyone is going to spread out and hunt for a small glass bottle and a grumpy rug. Right?'

'Right!' said Elf Girl.

'And when I say everyone,' said Raven Boy looking at Lord Socket. 'I mean everyone. Because I'm in charge now!'

Lord Socket didn't look too pleased, but he sighed and shrugged his shoulders.

'Come on then,' he said. 'Let's get on with it.'

So they did.

They searched the castle from top to bottom, even though Socket swore blind he hadn't pinched the tears or the rug.

Then everyone spread out over the town, and Raven Boy put them into groups of two and three, to hunt.

'This could take forever,' said Elf Girl.

'Do you have a better idea?' asked Raven Boy.

'Actually I do,' said Elf Girl. 'Not so much as an idea, more of a hunch.'

'A hunch?' said Raven Boy, but Elf Girl wasn't listening.

'Lord Socket,' she called. 'Don't you think we should find out what the Mayor's up to?'

Socket came striding over.

'Yes,' he said. 'You're right. If what you say about him is true . . . trolls!'

Socket waved at the three trolls, who trotted over, ready to bash anything or anyone, and the six of them raced through town, straight for the Mayor's house.

The first glimmer of dawn was starting to show behind the rooftops of Terror Town.

Soon, they reached the Mayor's front door.

Cedric was about to thump on the door, when Elf Girl put her finger to her lips and shook her head.

'Let's be smart about this,' she whispered, creeping up to a window and putting her pointy ear against it.

'There's someone in there. Two people at least. It sounds like they're having an argument.'

'Great,' said Cedric, and kicked the door in.

Elf Girl sighed.

The trolls roared into the house, and finding the ground floor empty, hurried upstairs.

Raven Boy and Elf Girl were right behind them, and Lord Socket followed, more cautiously.

The second floor was empty too. But still the sound of arguing came from somewhere.

'Shh!' hissed Elf Girl, and everyone stopped long enough for her to use her pointy ears properly.

Suddenly, she tilted her head and pointed up to the ceiling.

'He's on the roof!' she cried.

She was right.

All six of them clambered up the steps onto the roof to find the Mayor standing on the flying carpet. He held a small glass bottle,

and in front of him was Shona. They were having a blazing row.

'I order you to get me out of here!' the Mayor was yelling.

Shona had her hands on her hips. She was in a terrible mood.

'I will remind passengers again that any lack of respect on their part towards the staff and crew of the airline will be met with the strongest resistance.'

'You're just a rug! A flying rug, but a rug nonetheless!' shouted the Mayor.

'Stop! Stop right there!' cried Socket.

'I assure you,' said Shona, 'I do not fly at night without proper authorisation.' She glared at the Mayor again. 'And I remind you to behave yourself before I call the police!'

'The what?' said the Mayor. 'Listen, you'd better fly right now or I'll set fire to your tassels!'

He pulled a box of matches from his pocket and lit one, holding it near the tassels on the edge of the flying carpet.

'Ahh!' screamed Shona. 'All right! I'll do it. Just don't burn me!'

The carpet shot into the air, and raced into the night.

'Quick!' yelled Raven Boy. 'Get him!'

Elf Girl slipped her bow off her back, and took aim.

The carpet was already far away, and they could only really see it from the faint glow of the match that was making Shona fly when she didn't want to.

'You'll never hit it at this range!' cried Raven Boy.

'Shh!' hissed Elf Girl. 'I'm concentrating.'

She seemed to wait for ages, and the carpet got smaller and smaller. Raven Boy saw the arrow birthmark on her forearm glowing brightly, and then finally, she fired the magic bow.

What left the glowing magical bowstring wasn't an arrow, but a jet of water, that streaked into the night towards the carpet.

From a great distance, they saw the match go out, and heard a yelp as the Mayor got a soaking.

Shona the carpet wheeled around. Without anything to threaten her, she decided to return to the roof, where she landed while the Mayor tried to light another match, but they were as wet as he was, and he failed.

'You!' roared Socket. 'Are in a lot of trouble! Give these nice young people their bottle of water back, and get off that carpet right now!'

'And you!' cried Raven Boy to Elf Girl. 'Are amazing! That was brilliant!'

EIGHTEEN

**The world is full of magic
numbers. Like 3 and 7, but 9 is
the most magical number of all.
That's something that Raven
Boy and Elf Girl are about
to learn.**

The celebrations lasted until the next morning,
by which time the sun had come up shining
brightly, turning the three trolls back into men
for another day.

Socket had agreed to allow everyone to
sleep at the castle, just in case the Goblin King's
monsters made it through the gates again.

'But that shouldn't happen any more,'

said Socket to Elf Girl and Raven Boy. 'Thanks to you two.'

The Mayor had confessed. He said he'd seen Elf Girl and Raven Boy land on their magic carpet. He guessed the Tears of the Moon might be valuable and, at the very least, the rug would earn him a fortune. He explained that he'd been bewitched by the Goblin King into opening the gates of the town every night.

'Did you actually meet him?' asked Raven Boy, nervously.

'No,' said the Mayor. 'He came to me in a dream. He said he'd do terrible things to me if I didn't do what he asked.'

Raven Boy frowned. He turned to Lord Socket.

'What's to stop the Goblin King trying this out on someone else?'

'Nothing!' said Socket. 'Which is why your mission to defeat him must go ahead as soon as possible!'

'I was afraid you'd say that,' said Raven Boy.

He and Elf Girl asked for a day off first, during which time they mostly slept and ate whatever they could, all at Lord Socket's expense.

By the following morning, Raven Boy and Elf Girl knew it was time to set out once more. They gathered in the throne room, with Socket, Klingsor, Cedric, Bob and Bert, and many of the castle's inhabitants.

'We have everything we need now,' said Raven Boy. 'We have the Singing Sword.'

'Yes,' said Elf Girl. 'And you have to promise not to let it out of your hands while I'm around.'

'Even when I'm sleeping,' said Raven Boy. 'I know. We have the Singing Sword. And we have the Tears of the Moon back. It's time for the final part of our quest.'

He couldn't actually bring himself to say the words, 'And defeat the Goblin King', because he was so scared.

Elf Girl put her hand on his shoulder.

'I believe in you!' she said.

'So do I,' said Klingsor.

Socket looked thoughtful.

'You know,' he said.

166

'What you need is a little teamwork.'

'There's Elf Girl and me. We make a great team.'

'Hmm,' Socket said. 'Yes. But I wonder. Perhaps it might help you to take my wizard on your quest. Klingsor? What do you say?'

Klingsor looked horrified. He stared at Socket, and then he gave a deep sigh. He nodded.

'Who wants to live forever?' he said.

'That's very reassuring,' said Elf Girl, looking as if it was anything but that.

'And we're coming too!' said Cedric. 'Don't forget that.'

'And we have the cross carpet,' added Raven Boy. 'She'll be useful for a quick getaway.'

'If there is a getaway,' muttered Elf Girl.

'Shh,' said Raven Boy. 'That's seven of us.'

Rat gave the loudest squeak Raven Boy had ever heard him give.

'I mean eight! Eight! Of course.'

'But eight is no good,' said Klingsor.

'No?' asked Elf Girl. 'Why not?'

'Because eight is not a magic number. Nine is a magic number. We need nine pilgrims on our quest if we are to succeed.'

'We do?' asked Raven Boy.

'If we want to succeed, yes. You need to choose one more person to come with us.'

Raven Boy swallowed, and looked around the room. There was no other choice. He lifted his arm and pointed a finger at Lord Socket.

'I think you ought to come.'

'Now wait a minute . . .' began Socket, but Klingsor silenced him.

'The boy is in charge! You said so yourself.'

'I know, but . . .'

'But nothing! We need nine! The prophecy has spoken!'

'The prophecy? What prophecy? You didn't say anything about nine before!'

'You should have let me get to the second verse,' said Klingsor, grumpily. Then he grinned, and every wrinkle on every wrinkle seemed to smile with him.

'So! We have nine pilgrims, and we go to fight the Goblin King! To save the world and restore peace and good health!'

He winked.

'That's worth a cheer, isn't it?'

So everyone cheered, and they were still
cheering as the nine of them made their way out
of the castle gates, eight of them riding on the
the ninth, Shona the flying carpet.

'Just wait the Goblin King sees us!'
announced Raven Boy.

Elf Girl began sniggering.

'What?' asked Raven Boy.

'I can't help it,' said Elf Girl, snurking like she'd never snurked before.

'What?' demanded Raven Boy.

'I'm sorry,' said Elf Girl. 'But look at us! Three trolls, a decrepit wizard, a cowardly lord, a cheese-eating rodent and you and me.'

Raven Boy blinked.

'You forgot the grumpy carpet.'

Elf Girl's snurk turned into a proper giggle, and then she was snorting away so hard that Raven Boy thought she might fall off the rug.

But she didn't and soon he joined her, and they both rolled around, barely able to breathe, while the others looked on puzzled.

Rat squeaked, trying to tell them that this sort of thing happened all the time, but they didn't understood him, so he just jumped onto Raven Boy and began tickling him with his claws, for extra fun.

So, with Shona trying in vain to get her passengers to behave, they flew towards the horizon, heading for the Creepy Caves, and the final showdown with the Goblin King.

Next

Follow Raven Boy and Elf Girl (and Rat) as they make their way to CREEPY CAVES for a final showdown with the Goblin King.

Fright Forest

Monster Mountains

Scream Sea

Dread Desert

Terror Town

Creepy Caves

the orion star

★ ★ ★

CALLING ALL GROWN-UPS!
Sign up for **the orion star** newsletter to
hear about your favourite authors and exclusive
competitions, plus details of how children
can join our 'Story Stars' review panel.

Sign up at:

www.orionbooks.co.uk/orionstar

Follow us 🐦 @the_orionstar
Find us ⓕ facebook.com/TheOrionStar